The Librarian
A Life in Picture Books

by Linda Trott Dickman
Illustrated by Cydney Bittner

The Librarian - A Life in Picture Books

Copyright © 2024 Linda Trott Dickman

All rights reserved.

Published by Red Penguin Books

Bellerose Village, New York

ISBN
Print 978-1-63777-565-3 / 978-1-63777-566-0

No part of this book may be reproduced in any form or by any electronic or mechanical means, including information storage and retrieval systems, without written permission from the author, except for the use of brief quotations in a book review.

Dedication

For readers of picture books, who see beyond.
For the author and finisher of my faith.

Preface

My childhood was a magical one. I had parents who read to me every night, who purchased books for my brother and I, who told stories of their childhood and made-up stories when the occasion was ripe. Many folks I know left picture books behind as they grew, as they graduated to novels and different genres. I, too, was one of these, until I took a children's literature class in college. Our teacher was a great "Wild Thing," right out of the pages of Maurice Sendak's *Where the Wild Things Are*. She "rolled her terrible eyes, roared her terrible roar, gnashed her terrible teeth," and I was hooked. I stayed hooked and embraced a career as a children's librarian. Thousands of stories passed through my hands, were shared with children, were stored in my heart.

This collection represents a sampling of those picture books that influenced me, and I hope, will inspire you to read them all and write poems of your own.

Contents

Shhh!!! 1
A Child's Garden of ... 2
The Goops 3
Puss in Boots 4
The Most Beautiful Tree in the World 5
The Story about Ping 6
Harry the Dirty Dog 8
Madeline 9
Beauty and the Beast 10
The Sand Horse 12
Katy and the Big Snow 13
The Little House 14
Unspoken 16
The Magical, Mystical, Marvelous Coat 17
Pockets 19
The Rough-Face Girl 20
Oh, Great Spirit 23

Make Way for Ducklings 24
The 500 Scats of Kevin Carroll 26
The Giving Tree 29
Pumpkin Moonshine 30
The Sea Chest 31
Home 32
The Storytelling Princess 34
Swan Song 35
The King of Ireland's Son 36
The Valentine Bears 38
Scare, Crow 40
The Clown of God 41
How Jo the Bear and T the Mouse Got Together 42
A Partita on Sleeping Beauty 44
And They Lived 46
Acknowledgements: 55
The Reading List 56

Shhh!!!

The library is a quiet place.
Don't you know you can't
sing and dance?
Walking on the tables is strictly
forbidden.
Dress up clothes?
A hat rack?
You must be crazy!
Shh!!
Oh.
What?
You're who?

The Librarian?
Oops.

1

A Child's Garden of …

inspired by The Land of Counterpane by R.L. Stevenson

When I was sick, and lay abed
my Mimi doll heard all I said.
She heard my secrets and my fears
and ne'er let on, o'er all those years.

Mimi and an armadillo
Great-grandma made – a little pillow
teal with black yarn eyes sewn in,
Emily's craft, my comfort then.

A host of dollies, all my mother's
arrayed in country costumes, others
paraded all around the sheets
flashing color, runway feats.

My matchbox cars were way too small
to hold the dolls, and still they crawled
up and over sheets, up over dollies
so much fun, the sick day follies.

The Goops
inspired by Gelett Burgess

It happened every evening
when I was just a girl.
We'd peel the blue book open
pearly pages we'd unfurl.

We'd reach the golden inset
you'd read to me aloud
all about ill manners
that the Goops forever showed.

I memorized that poem
We'd recite it, loud and clear
then slam the book, say prayers, sleep tight
knowing you were near.

And then when at the table
you'd give me that look
I'd remember what came next
just waiting for that book.

Puss in Boots
for Charles Perrault
for Margarette Wahl

It never occurred to me
that a cat could not be an advocate.
This cat was clever, had a velvet tongue
boots that were made for walking.

That a cat could promote,
support, extol his master's virtue,
talk his master's way
right into the kingdom,
never an impossibility, I thought.

Puss fended off the biggest, scariest ogre
whoever filled a swirling stone stairway,
waiting for me with every page turn.
I was terrified. Loved the ending,
scared of the ogre.

But I had my own defender
who was in no wise a cat,
and saved me
by simply teaching me to turn the page.

The Most Beautiful Tree in the World

for Leonard Weisgard
for the Rockefeller Center Christmas Tree

It stood there, center stage on the cover,
bejeweled in lights and ornaments
for all the world to see.

The long trip took little toll,
her last days had begun
with that first cut.

Cut from home and comfort
transported by truck o'er country roads,
suspension bridges,
for one final public performance.
Primped and pampered for her opening night,
raised up, overlooking skaters and angels,

that fueled this little girl's dreams.

The Story about Ping
for Marjorie Flack

He knew he was late
he feared the spank on his back
he watched his brothers and sisters
he watched his aunts and uncles
he watched his cousins make their way
to the little bridge and march
onto the wise-eyed boat.
He did not want the spank,
so, he hid.

Alone, in the grasses, hidden.
He knew he was lost
he entered the sunlight
he entered the water
he entered the crowd of cormorants
saw them, catching
but not eating their treasure, rewarded
by their master with bits of fish.

There was a trail.
He followed the crumbs
he followed the rice cakes
he followed the boy,
a small boat boy, proud of his prize,
showing Ping to his large family.
He was contained in a basket where the sun
found windows to color the deck.
He was a hoped-for dinner.

The basket rose, he was set free.

The basket lifted by the same little boy.
The basket that was no longer his prison.
Just in time to hear the call
from the Wise-Eyed boat,
see the line of family.

Ping still feared the spank,
he took his place at the end.
This was one bridge
he was ready to cross.

Harry the Dirty Dog

for all the dirty dogs, and kids,
for Charlotte Zolotow

Harry was a white dog with black spots
the sound of running water
a signal to run.
Harry hated getting a bath.
Harry hated it so much
that he hid the scrubbing brush,
ran away from home.

Each place he roamed
made him dirty
dirtier
and dirtier still.
He became a black dog,
with white spots.

A dog who was tired,
hungry, missing his family.
He ran home,
snuck into the backyard,
called out. He was
a stranger to them.

Uncovering the buried
bristled treasure, he bounded
to the tub happily barking
and hopped
in, holding the brush
in his mouth.

He became a white dog
with black spots
once more, dreaming
about all the fun
it was getting dirty.

There is renewed hope
for me.

Madeline

inspired by Ludwig Bemelmans

There was no house in Paris
covered in vines,
no twelve little girls
just yours, just mine.

We sat at table
broke our bread
then teeth were brushed
and off to bed.

Off to bed with a smile
and a prayer,
a favorite toy
was always there.

We had no Miss Clavel to wake
t'was Mom or Dad when wee ones quaked
Dad, whose hearing never failed
when little ones, in sleep would wail.

Whether lullabye or rocking chair
Mom or Dad were always there
to wipe a tear, to soothe a brow.
Pop-pop, Grandma knew just how

to soothe the parent, soothe the baby
on the brink of sleep. Just maybe
they had been there oft before
now at the rescue at our door.

Two little girls in no straight line
danced, and sang and turned out fine.

Beauty and the Beast
for all the undiscovered Beasts and Beauties

All she asked for was a rose,
no silk, no pearls, did she request.
Off went Father to ply his trade
off went Father, his fortune made.

Bare and barer, no ships awaited,
turn around, his heart restore.
Poorer than poor was now his fate
perchance, a rose, he couldn't do more.

Lost along the road at night
tethered horse to manger near.
Went inside rooms burning bright
found all that might welcome there.

Night and day, and no host shew*
but breakfast warm and fresh he ate.
Thanked aloud his host, withdrew
back to the road, tell of his state.

While he gathered, to make his way,
he espied a rose bush pale.
He thought of her, his Beauty bright
cut one rose just beside the trail.

Beast emerged, so loud and fierce
took him pris'ner for his crime.
Gave him leave to make his peace
unless a daughter return in time.

Beauty came back in exchange
her Father's life was her reward.
In time she met the Beast so strange
she stayed there of her own accord.

Parting sorrows, courage met
her greatest wish she spoke aloud.
That she might see her family yet
a magic mirror, to her it showed.

Over time they came to know
an ease that friendship can enjoy.
All the while, a ticking clock
worked against Beast, stole his joy.

As his time came near its end,
Beauty, on a trip so dear
saw her Beast, to sorrow bend
and to his side, returned she there.

Her heart had turned, where friendship grew
tender love, did pierce heart's ground.
Her intent then she made known,
and Beauty, her true station found.

We found each other long ago
beauties, beasts, we'd both known well.
Uncovered what was good and true
we stand together, in heaven dwell.

* Shew – showed up, presented themself

The Sand Horse

after the Sand Horse by Ann Turnbull
for my father-in-law, who always wanted to fly

He was afraid of the water.
His family looked to the bay:
"Horses! White horses," called the artist's wife.
White manes of equines tossed their heads, waving.

Sand artist, inspired to build.
A herd of pails hauled from the sea
neat and slow,
developed, appreciated, muscles
hooves, one mane rippling.

Artist's work over
time for the magic of the sea.

Revelation came to the horse, he awoke,
sensed the others, let the sea take him
everywhere he always wanted to be,
just like you, Dad.

Katy and the Big Snow

after Katy and the Big Snow by Virginia Lee Burton
for my husband

Katy loved her work.
The Highway Department of Geopolis
kept her busy summer and winter
bulldozing, plowing.
Fifty-five horses pulling together
working together.
Traffic flowed.

The harder and tougher the job
the happier Katy worked.
She was their pride and joy.
Winter kept her bound, for all her power.
Until the big snow.

One by one business, services, roads
closed.
Everything.
Stopped.
But.
Katy.

Katy dug through
the thickness, leading
police, postmaster, railway,
communications - the roads
east, north, west and south
all the way to the airport.
The city was unveiled,
thanks to Katy.

Just like you broke through the
snowdrifts
to find
me.

The Little House

inspired by Virginia Lee Burton
for Grandma Gozelski's woods

Once upon a time
there was an orchard
on a pretty little hill
right across from Mrs. G's woods.

The farmer sold the land,
Orchard Farms was born,
and so was the little girl
who moved into 436.

The little girl was very happy
at 436. She made friends
played baseball with the boys
and girls in the neighborhood.

They played in the backwoods,
built forts, played tight rope
on the log over the gully.

By and by,
the little girl moved to 1951,
on a Navy base in California.
She loved California,
she missed 436.

She was growing up.
436 was always home.
The White Mountains called her
 to go away to college.
She was always joyful to come home
to 436, which welcomed her,
like an old friend.

She married, went back to school
the White Mountains offered
no protection against *his* darkness.
436 sent a hero to rescue her,
bring her home once more.
Just a remnant of Mrs. G's woods left.

Number 8 was her first solo apartment
until the pond decided to trickle in.
Easter found her back at 436,
healing, getting ready to leave once more.
She left in a flurry of white and rain,
married 10 Brittany.

They moved to 393, then to 41,
436 remained her anchor.
Everything else came and went.

Her sailor dad and his only mate passed.

Slowly
41
moved
to
436.

Their two little girls
played,
made friends at school,
babysat for the neighbors
and bonded
with the people
who lived in the farm house
where the orchard began
right across from Mrs. G's woods.

Unspoken

for Henry Cole
for those who escaped
for those who helped them

I know you could hear me
breathing in the sheaves.
I saw the quilt. But still
I was scared. Too scared
to even breathe, until
I got into the cornstalks.

That's when you came in.
Your kitty knew. She could smell me
in among the tall stalks.
You ran, I know you were scared too.
You heard the soldiers
but not too scared to care.

Not too scared to wrap muffins,
still warm from the oven,
in that checkered napkin.
Every crumb a feast.
Cornbread, pie, potato, chicken wing.
For five days, you found a way.
Even when that soldier came.

That's why I made the doll,
a little bit of warmth in the napkin
a little bit of smile in the cornstalk
the smell of freedom
as close as inhale,
as sweet as the Big Dipper.

The Magical, Mystical, Marvelous Coat

for Catherine Ann Cullen and her magical, mystical, marvelous story

It had been a long week, all my buttons were lost
my momma, unhappy, spoke to me of the cost.
How to replace them? How to find more?
And then, we both heard it, a rap at the door.

All six creatures I'd helped stood there with a smile
asking if they could come in, stay a while
thankful for buttons: cold, warm, tune, star, stone,
and doll– all were helpful, their eyes now bright shone.

That Sunday, upstairs with the crowd I did go,
My buttons restored, from the heel to the throat.
I ran my hand upward from "cold" to the "doll"
found yet one more button, that babbled and called.

It was the color of cerulean blue
I touched it and wondered "Just what do you do?"
The mirror reflected a button that showed
water that moved and appeared to, well, flow.

Soon we went for a walk to see what we'd see
We found a sad child, just looking at me,
I pinched off blue button, put it in her hand.
Refreshed, squared her shoulders, and smiling, did stand.

The button replenished, like drops from the sky,
Each one that it touched, new hope now drew nigh
Reviving again, and again, and again.
That magical button, whose reach did extend.

My magical, mystical, marvelous coat,
Oh its buttons that run from the heel to the throat
Has a seventh that makes all the others to shine,
to share not just marvelous, but truly divine.

Pockets

for Jennifer Armstrong
for my blue-eyed honey

She was washed up on the prairie
bereft of all
but slumbering vision.

Moving among the grays,
stolid blues of the people's garments.
She heard their woes,
saw their sad displeasures
a simple seamstress she.

Each garment that came to her hand,
each waistcoat,
each shirtwaist,
each pair of pantalones -
she enriched their pockets.
French knots, running stitches,
satin, feather, herringbone stitches.
Turning their hopes into threaded
talismans, embroidered texture and touchstones
against their travails.

Stitch by stitch,
pocket by pocket,
the sullen, creased expressions upturned,
they found hope, golden dreams, love anew
the town transformed
a colorful oasis on the prairie,
the very prairie where she unfurled
new sails, now awash with color.

Just as You filled my sails
with the wind of Your Spirit.

The Rough-Face Girl

for Rafe Martin, and the Invisible Being
for my own little duckling

Painted with the sun, moon, stars,
plants, trees and animals, the wigwam
rested upon the shores of Lake Ontario.

In it, lived the Invisible Being,
who was said to be great, rich,
powerful, handsome and sought after.
One rule only: you must be able to see him.

Maidens, seeking him, engaged
with his sister, whose vision lacked
nothing, whose questions probed,
deeply.

A motherless family lived
in the village. Older sisters,
cruel to their younger, cast
her closest to the fire, tending
it and their needs.

Hair charred; face scarred
hands marred, burnt arms, spirit scored
by unkindness, they called her
Rough-face Girl. Their only
other contribution, misery.

Sisters lied their way inside,
they were blinded by foolishness,
seeing nothing. Seeing nothing,
sent away.
Finery demanded, their father
had little left but his sandals.

Rough-face girl saw nothing
but him, in the rainbow, in the stars,
in the beauty of creation. Finery
depleted, her resourcefulness
gained scorn from all who cast
their gaze upon her. Making her way

to the wigwam, birch bark dress
carved with symbols of sun,
moon, stars, plants, trees, animals.
She flap, flap, flapped like duck's
feet as she walked, determined
at every turn.
At every turn, he was all she saw.

Walked on, walked up, welcomed in.
Sister greeted her warmly,
began the interview. "What makes his bow?"
"What makes the runner of his sled?"
Her answers – her vision celebrated
her beauty seen by both.

Sent to the waters of Ontario,
her splendor, unsheathed,
arrayed in heavenly garment.
Married, they lived in gladness.

I still have the sandals.

Oh, Great Spirit
prayer of Rough Face Girl

I follow your way,
see your bow after rain,
see your sled in the night,
trail of light guiding me.

I want to shake off the ashes
let the outer scars begin
their heal. My sisters' desire
to marry your son.

They are not alone.
All the maidens adorn
sashay, strut, prance
making their claim
saying your name.

No selfless hues,
visions dim.
Forgive them.

I am not one
to deny desires
of my own.

I have no finery
but the work of my hands
using what you provide
to make my covering,
seeking my father's help.

Walking in his shoes
on my way to see
what you and your sister
already knew
could be.

Make Way for Ducklings
inspired by Robert McCloskey

Mr. and Mrs. Flyer looked
all over the island for a home.
They looked to the West,
but Mr. Flyer did not want
the sun in his eyes
in his morning flight path.

They looked to the East,
but there was such a distance
from Mr. Flyer's home.
He considered the winters,
looked again at the landscape.

He did look again, using
a compass and an airplane.
Within a circle they chose
a place east of work,
just enough west to clear
one's head on the commute.

Little ones came along,
Mrs. Flyer would walk
the girl and push the boy.
One day, while on a long walk,
they began to cross the street.
The girl ran out ahead of Mrs. Flyer.

That caused Mrs. Flyer to throw
herself between the girl
and an oncoming car.
Whew! They were safe.
They were always safe
with Mr. and Mrs. Flyer.

The girl and the boy learned.
Mr. Flyer was wise and kind,
lived to tell stories.
Mrs. Flyer was protective,
loved to sing and dance.
These too, were good tools.
The Flyers made friends
with all the merchants,
and all the neighbors.

They knew how to watch,
listen, and just how to offer
a drink of water on a hot day.
All the neighbors watched
out for the many children.

Mr. and Mrs. Flyer's ducklings
grew and grew.
He made music,
she wrote words.
She made music,
he sang the words.
They found mates,
homes and had their own little ducks.

They kept on widening the circle,
spreading the joy of family
far beyond their borders...

The 500 Scats of Kevin Carroll

after The 500 Hats of Bartholomew Cubbins
for Theodore Geisel and Ella Fitzgerald
for Kevin Carroll and Don Sherman

The Kingdom of Portnorth
right there near the bay
made its residents swell
with their swing and their sway.

Folks gathered each summer
right down in the park
for grand evening concerts
held there after dark.

They'd all bring their strollers
their blankets and such
spread out on the green
it all was too much!

With ice cream from Sweet Shop
Rocking Horse or Lics
they'd saunter on down
for a musical fix.

One day as King Mayor
was walking along,
a small Portnorth boy
was caught singing his song.

He sang it out loud
and he sang it out soft
when the concert, near ready
he could not turn it off.

"Please stop," said the King
and the boy closed his mouth
but the song kept on coming,
of notes were no drouth.*

*drought

He walked with the King
right down to the park.
"Stop singing please child."
But the prospects were dark.

The notes kept on coming,
the notes did not stop
the notes ranged in sound
from scale bottom to top.

"Why aren't you stopping child,
I am the King!"
"I'm trying," he sang,
and his hands, he did wring.

He stopped up his ears
thinking that might be some help.
but the notes found their way
through that musical whelp.

The King grew impatient
his frustration grew, grew, grew.
"Do you know who is asking?
I'm the King that is who!"

"I know you your majesty,
make no mistake,
if I could stop singing
my knees wouldn't shake."

"Such impudence son
I shall call out the guard.
Just simply stop singing.
It can't be that hard."

A crowd was now gathering
around the duet.
The King saying "Quiet!"
the song would not abet.

They got nearer the bandstand
Don Sherman just looked.
His baton stopped mid-air
to this tune, he was hooked.

"This child," said King Mayor,
will not stop his singing.
"No matter the ask,
this tune he keeps swinging."

The band stopped their playing
the people stopped talking
King Mayor shrugged shoulders
to the bandstand kept walking.

The conductor tilted his head
over to the side
and then came a grin
that was so very wide.

"This child, dear King Mayor
has brought us the tune
for the tribute to *you*
we've been stuck on since noon!"

He sang it once more,
he sang it out loud
"Got it," said the conductor.
The lad stood so proud.

"King Mayor, sweet youngster,"
he said with a grin.
"Our tribute is settled.
Let the concert begin."

The conductor tap-tapped his baton
then he raised it
his arms held like wings
every music eye gazed it.

When down came his arms
they came down, just like that
and the young man continued
to scat scat scat scat.

At the end of the piece
at the end of his song
the mayor rejoiced
joined the wee one in song.

Down at the bandstand
when the wind is just right
you can hear breezes scatting
right into the night.

The Giving Tree

for Shel Silverstein
Loves like a hurricane, I am a tree – David Crowder

It had to come down you know –
it stood for over 60 years
budding, flowering, greening,
colored by autumn's breath,
shedding, leaves raked, jumped in.

Then, a branch here, a branch there,
harshly pruned by cyclones, a gas leak
escaping to poison, discolor, disintegrate.

Finally, a branch fell
on a calm, clear sunny day
and we knew.
Called the tree guy.
It was dying
infested with carpenter ants

who ruthlessly tore
at the core
with no thought of rebuilding, improving.
No thought but to destroy
from the inside out —
nothing at all like you, Jesus,
nothing at all.

Pumpkin Moonshine

for Mary Jane Scott,
for the sweet wee person, Tasha Tudor

One stood so tall, so tall, so tall
towering over the students
seated and standing.
Sharing treasures, burnished
marble smooth, covers rounded,
illustrations tipped –in.

When she read *Where the Wild Things Are*
she roared her terrible roar
gnashed her terrible teeth,
rolled her terrible eyes,
showed her terrible claws

except this one time.
In walked a sweet, wee, person
so small, so small, so small.
Seated and standing
we towered over her.

Sharing Tasha treasures,
burnished-marble-smooth,
covers wee and rounded, illustrations,
hand lettering her own.

Together they redefined Sylvie Ann
and Pumpkin Moonshine
cherished all.

The Sea Chest

for Sarah Han
for Toni Buzzeo

You did not come by boat,
or car or train.
There was no shipwreck,
no sealed and bound sea chest containing
your precious life.

You were coming.
We made preparations.
Oh! Celebrations!
Off to the airport
chatting with other expectants.

You came with your *dol-bok*.
adorned with your name, accompanied,
wrapped round in a greeting quilt,
locked on by your new brother,
his joy uncontained.

Your parents loved you so much
they were willing
to cast you upon a new country,
a new family.

We did not name you Windborne,
but we could have.

Home
for Thomas Locker

Planted, as a tree by the waters
he brushed with life daily.

 Storm King, overseeing
the invincible river.
Tom captured it,
carried it, was baptized by-
the almighty Hudson.

It was his story,
It was his song,
painting the Hudson
all the day long.

Discovered by a young one
in a small library,
on a *Sound* not far
from Hudson's mouth,
a poem was written,
a phone call received,
a meeting planned.

Transplanted for a day,
the sky was colored *Hudson River School*
that he might draw on its strength

and find his way
home.

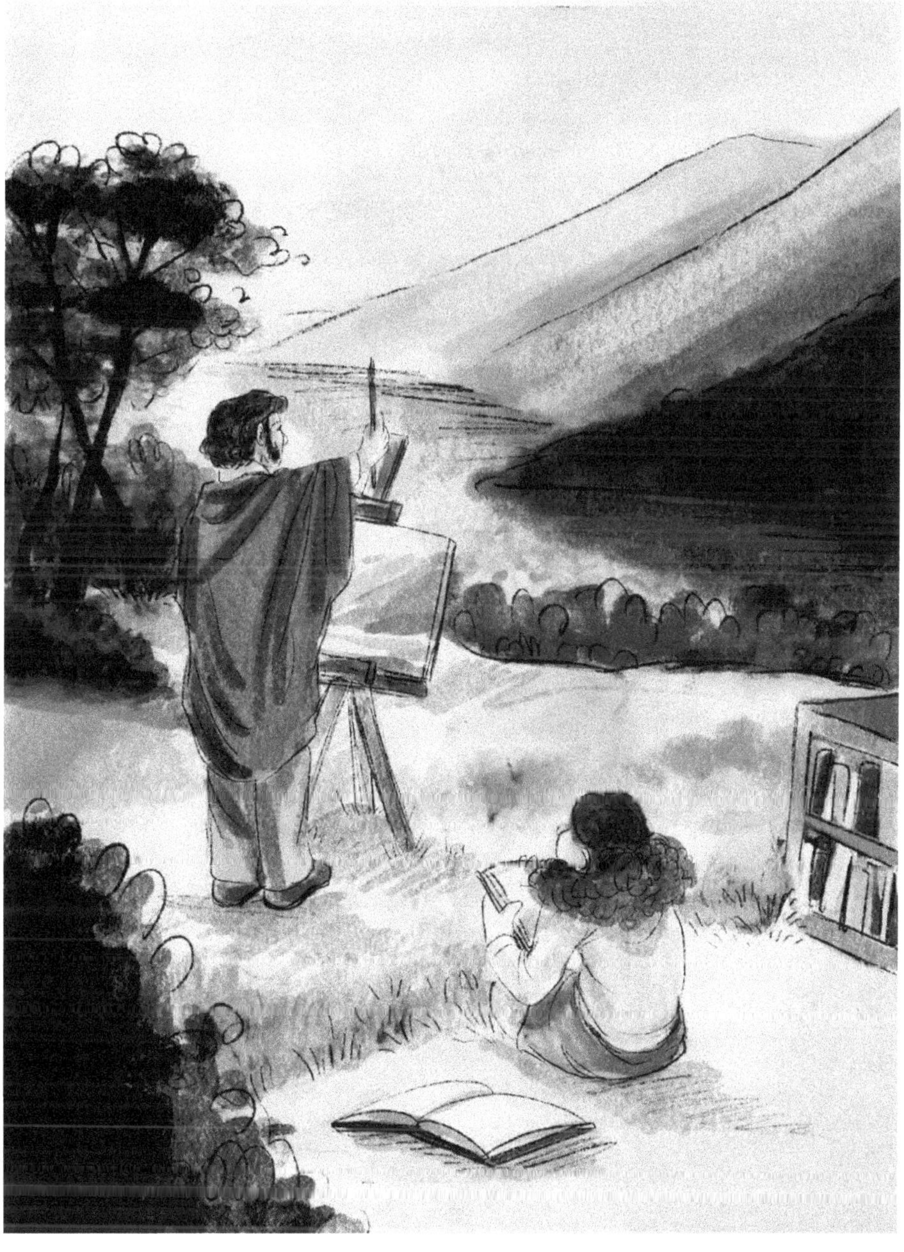

The Storytelling Princess

for Rafe Martin
and for the cavalier teacher...

Dad was always telling me
I should go to the Presbyterian Church,
the one in Northport.
I should meet a professional man.
I would have none of it.
I had to do it on my own.

I wrote out a prayer,
a list of the things that were absolutely
a priority. I prayed on it. Literally.
Then spent too many years trying
to help God fill the list.

He was set up, with a nice red-headed girl
whose parents were ministers,
whose grandparents had braved the west
in wagons, or buckboards, or something.
He asked if he could bring a friend along
on the sailing date.

No one was prepared for me.
With my one strapped, polka-dotted
bathing suit, my Mulligan Stew faith
journey,
my Catholic roots, my previous marriage.

We played out our story at Radio Shack,
with Tom and Jane Sawyer taking classic
notes.
He was the cavalier teacher,
I was the matronly student.

The matronly librarian
who married the cavalier teacher
at the Presbyterian Church in Northport.

Swan Song

for all the enchanted swans
for those who weave

She looked around the darkened room,
the small book-company box
self-lid, closing uncomfortably
on sleeves of completed plans.

She held the book, created
just for her, as if the authors
were in her embrace.

All that traveling, across
the realm, surviving wicked
witches, often in silence
for the sake of the children.

Weaving her tales, like flaxen
coverings, taking the stings
with eyes toward Heaven.

One last thing remained;
the partially finished shirt
in the shadowbox.

She kept her silence,
stayed one more year
weaving until they were free.

The King of Ireland's Son
for Brendan Behan and Robert "Himself" McKenna

T'was the heavenly music that started it all.
The King of Ireland sent out his sons he did.
The tricksy older brothers
promising to pull their youngest brother.

Didja' think I did not know?
You met the old men,
ate and drank only the best brew
the finest crubeens, fresh soda bread,
yellow buck porridge.
Still, you had a-ways to go.

The oldest man told you
to look for me, and you're a good lad
you did what you were told,
all in an effort to find the heavenly music.

You found me at the end of the road,
and I brought you as far as I could.
You met the surly man that held her captive,
you answered honestly
when he put you to the test, you did.

The challenge was laid out,
you told the old fool
you'd like to see yer stallion,
and here we are.

You put yer left hand in my right ear
found the tablecloth, ye spread
it out ye did. I told you to put your right
hand into me left ear and oh didn't we eat?

In the morning, you found the old fool
just where I told you. After he finished
his roar, he set before you a new puzzle,
and ye came back to me, didn't you now?

After a fine feast, and good rest,
you went back. The old giant
hid himself in a football.
You kicked him out and wasn't
he nasty? We had a fine feed
and I taught you sign language
fer yer last task.

In the morning, the daughter
of the King of Greece sang away,
nodding you toward the hearth
she did, telling you to take her ring
and toss it there.
Now it t'was your turn to hide

and hide you did, three times 'round
the sun you went, and three times
he couldn't find yer.
All the while we ate and drank like kings,
the giant was out of his mind to find ye.

Find you he did not. He nearly went
demented. You broke the spell!
The daughter of the King of Greece
and yourself, rode out into the light
the King of Ireland got his heavenly music
and you and herself were married,
and wasn't it a fine feast after all?

Trapped was I, in my own hurt,
in my own help, in my own way.
Forgot how to sing fer a bit,
and who I should sing to.

But I got His signal,
heard yer own song,
we found our way back
to the salt air, to each other.
A fine feast indeed.

The Valentine Bears

for my own Softbear
for Eve Bunting

Mrs. Bear and Mr. Bear
rarely shared a winter day.
Hibernation got in the way.

Mrs. Bear set the clock
for half past winter, Valentine's.
She planned a special, waking time.

The alarm went off,
Mr. Bear just kept snoring.
She went off to do her choring.

Stored up his favorite
fresh-made jam, strawberry,
and peanut butter, smooth and merry.

Wrote a poem or two or three
about the love that came to be,
years ago, between he and she.

Placed the poems, set the table,
went to wake him up, no luck.
He kept snoring, covers tucked.

She tugged his ear; she kissed his eyes.
Nothing. All she heard were snorts,
mumbling strange new words, all sorts.

She couldn't wait, she went outside
filled a tin with icy stream
went back in, to disturb his dream.

He popped up! Surprise, surprise!
She spilled the water on her dress.
They both helped to clean up the mess.

Laughter shared the day, so sweet
peanut butter, jam and chocolate too.
Kisses, poems and hugs a few.

Back to sleep until the spring.
Their first Valentine's success
smiling, snoring, together, pressed.

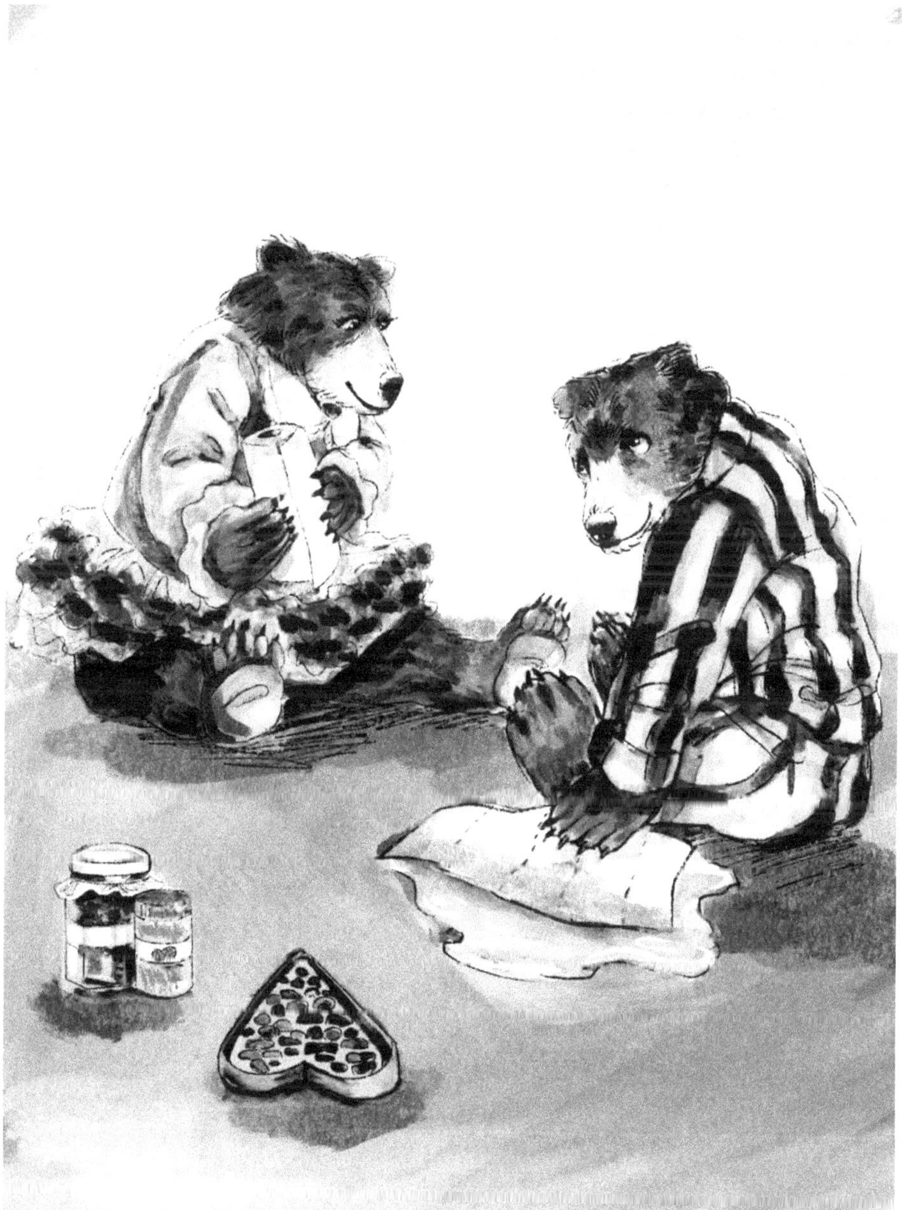

Scare, Crow

for Taro Yashima
 and all the Crow Boys

Chibi was missing, every day a scare
afraid of the teacher,
afraid of the children
alone, but for the sounds of the crow.

Alone at play, alone at study times, cared
only for the ceiling, the desk top,
the wet window pane,
the pattern on the shirt in front - crow

black. The bugs that gave others a scare
he knew, handled. He listened
to sounds near and far
end of line tag along - toxic row.

The others called him stupid, brusque air.
He crossed his eyes to unsee
passing him by. Slowpoke
they taunted to the back row.

Lunch, rice ball wrapped in radish leaves, care
to be in school each day for years.
New teacher took notice, spoke
kindly, smiled, cheered him, drastic row

change. Then a show, a stage, a stare, no scare.
Chibi got up, sharing song of the crow
cry of the crow, joy of the crow
tree-top lonely old crow.

They heard, no fears, care.
Now, shame, epiphany, tears.
Chibi no more.
Now Crow Boy.

The Clown of God

for Tomie dePaola

Your face is gonna freeze like that.
She always said it when I was making a
sour puss.
Sticking out my tongue,
kicking and screaming and crying.

Your face is gonna freeze like that.
Then I heard about the *Clown of God*,
who juggled colored balls,
painted a smile on his face,
saved the golden ball for last.

He was poor, homeless, popular
for a time, always saving *the sun*,
the golden ball for last.

When his dexterity failed,
he was scorned, reviled,
kept his smile, just once more,
for a special Mother and Child.

Just once more.
He tossed the golden sun,
his reward reflected on the child's face.
The clown's face froze like that.

I resolved to smile more.

How Jo the Bear and T the Mouse Got Together

for Beatrice Schenck de Regniers, and Theresa and Joanna

Call me Jo.
Call me T.

I am looking for a house.
I am looking for an apartment.
I love the East Coast.
I love the West Coast.

We cannot live together.
No, we cannot live together.

I like to take walks,
I like to take walks.
We can walk together!
I walk at the park at night.
I walk at the park in the morning.

We can't walk together.
No, we can't walk together.

I like music.
I like music.
We can play music together!
I like flute outside.
I like piano inside.
We cannot play music together.
We cannot play music together.

I love to create
I love to create.
I create stories, and knit things.
I create graphics and design things.
We create together.
Yes, we do create together.

Hi T.
Hi Jo.
What are you doing now?
It's Sunday, I am getting
ready for popcorn and ice cream.
I*t is Sunday, I am getting ready*
for popcorn and ice cream.

What kind of ice cream?
Oh I eat all kinds.
I eat all kinds too!

So, every Sunday, Jo the Bear
Yes, every Sunday, T the Mouse
have popcorn and ice cream, together,
one on the east coast,
one on the west coast.
enjoying each other, and a movie!

Wait, what movie?

A Partita on Sleeping Beauty

the scent of patchouli thickened the closer
she got
the turn of that strange coal black disc
she moved closer
held in the gaze of that singular eye
this sound had Mesmer

it wasn't in the stare
it wasn't in the spin
it wasn't in the climb that she made
against the din
it wasn't in the stars
it wasn't in the moon
it was only just because she sought to
change the tune

the lyric like a pheromone, she reached
toward the arm that rode atop the licorice
platter
held in the perfume of the disturbing
melody
this song made no scents,
but its taste, fresh cranberry on her
tongue

it wasn't in the air
though the room began to spin
a view she drank and held, for so long it
called her in

it wasn't in the stars
it wasn't in the moon
it was only just because she sought to
change the tune

reaching for the tonearm
the plinth's magnetic waves
her finger pierced
blood dropped, she fell,
drowsy with determination.
her song stilled the kingdom for a
century
What grew was expectancy,
what died was resistance
this song would wound

all along the air
danced with dust and ash
revived in evening dew
like aloe, closed a gash

it was not in the stars
it was not in the moon
it was in her desire to change that weary
tune

And They Lived

for all the other picture books that transform when the lights go out in the library
for all those transformed by them

The last bus had jettisoned
the lights were closed
the doors locked,
the library was dark.

The whisper began
Hum that apple, shoot that pea!
And backdoor the bum!

Just down the wall, Wild Things
Roared their terrible roars,
gnashed their terrible teeth,
rolled their terrible eyes.

Pumpkin Moonshine prevailed
over the night as **Harold and His Purple Crayon** created new adventures,
took great risks.

Tuesday, 8 pm frogs
rose up, flew through the night,
the laundry, the house, chased
the dog, lost altitude, not attitude.

Black as coal, Harry
the Dirty Dog was weary.
He began his journey home.

The Bottom lines:
"Play ball!" and everybody did.
And so today, there is baseball
in America once again.
There is still winter, but now
There is spring and autumn too.
And there are still jobs to do.
Only now, some of them
are at the ballpark.

And it was still hot.

The vines grew up and ran all over the cornfield,
with lots of pumpkins on them,
just waiting to be made into pumpkin pies
and pumpkin moonshines
to please good little girls like Sylvie Ann.

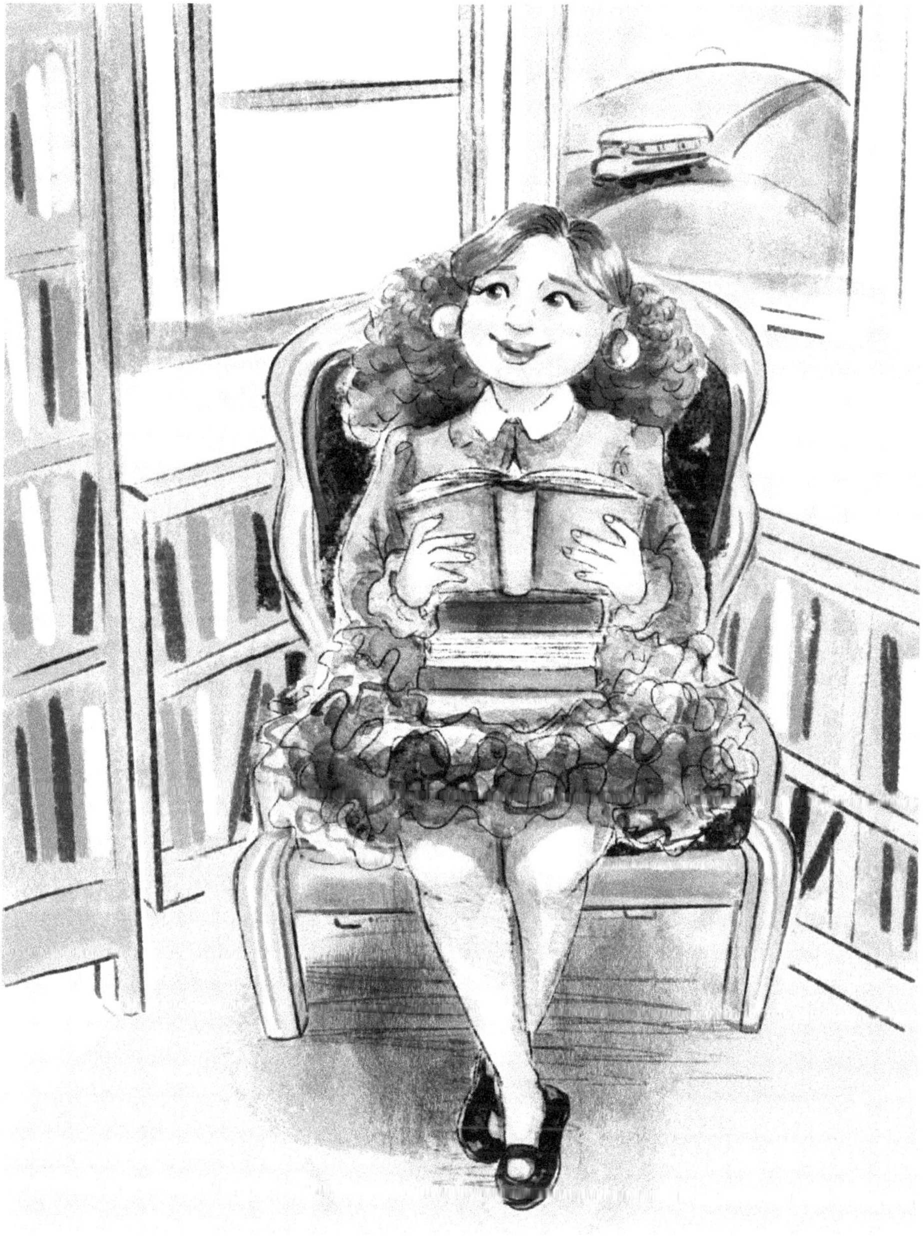

*The purple crayon dropped on the floor
and Harold dropped off to sleep.*

Wednesday, 8 pm

*He slept so soundly,
he didn't even feel the scrubbing brush under his pillow.*

Doors opened, lights on.
There was a trace of peanuts, hot dogs in the air,
a hint of moonglow across the carpet,
a shift in the eyes of the Wildest Thing of all,
a purple crayon, paper shed, on the floor.
And a whiff of clean dog.

The Librarian sat in her chair, ready
for the new day's characters.

The Reading List

The 500 Hats of Bartholomew Cubbins by Ted Geisel inspired
    "The 500 Scats of Kevin Carroll"
Beauty and the Beast by Gabrielle-Suzanne Barbot de Villeneuve
A Child's Garden of Verses by Robert Louis Stevenson
The Clown of God by Tomie DePaola
Crow Boy by Taro Yashima inspired "Scare, Crow"
The Giving Tree by Shel Silverstein
The Goops From Manners by Gelett Burgess
Harry the Dirty Dog by Charlotte Zolotow
Home- A Journey Through America by Thomas Locker Home – inspired "Home"
How Georgie Radbourn Saved Baseball by David Shannon
How Joe the Bear and Sam the Mouse Got Together by Beatrice Schenk De Regniers
Katy and the Big Snow by Virginia Lee Burton
The King of Ireland's Son by Brendan Behan
The Little House by Virginia Lee Burton
Madeline by Ludwig Bemelmans
The Magical, Mystical, Marvelous Coat by Catherine Ann Cullen
Make Way for Ducklings by Robert McCloskey
The Most Beautiful Tree in the World by Leonard Weisgard

Pockets by Jennifer Armstrong

Pumpkin Moonshine by Tasha Tudor

Puss in Boots by Kathryn Jackson

The Rough-Face Girl by Rafe Martin

The Sand Horse by Ann Turnbull

The Sea Chest by Toni Buzzeo

Sleeping Beauty by Charles Perrault

The Story about Ping by Kurt Wiese

The Storytelling Princess by Rafe Martin

Unspoken by Henry Cole

The Valentine Bears by Jan Brett

Where the Wild Things Are by Maurice Sendak

The Wild Swans by Hans Christian Andersen

Acknowledgements:

Thank you to all the authors whose works inspired this collection. Some of you are living, some have passed, I loved you all between the covers of your stories and in my own.

Thank you to my husband, my first editor, my faithful critic, my standard of excellence.

Thank you to my daughters, Theresa and Joanna who are and have always been my cheerleaders, and my son-in-law Dave whose support is always felt.

Thank you to Stephane Sands Larkin for believing in me and for her bright, unfailing support and laughter.

Thank you always and forever to Jacqueline Jones LaMon, to Judith Baumel, to Igor Webb, professors of excellence.

Thank you to Brendan McEntee for his relentless support and commentary.

Thank you to Rick Christiansen for his gentle words and courageous life.

Thank you to J R Turek, wise, wonderful, dog-loving editor and purple poet, whose support lifts me always.

Meet Poet Linda Trott Dickman

Since the age of three, I always wanted to teach. One summer, my mother found me lining children of all ages up on a split rail fence, and "teaching" them while she was just inside the laundromat door in a Laconia, New Hampshire.

That desire moved on to teaching kids how to dive from a kneeling position on the sides of many a pool from here to California and back. I turned my dream of teaching into a reality when I graduated from Plymouth State College (now University) in Plymouth, NH with a degree that would enable me to teach in a one room schoolhouse. That gave me the necessary links between grade levels, subject matter, to see how a subject might grow from Kindergarten through High School.

Then I became a librarian when I saw that I could have my two great loves together: children and books! This further strengthened the connections between curriculum areas. For over forty years I served both public and school libraries.

It is my hope that this book will gather people together, to share their favorite stories, to read the books on this list and add to it. That would give me as much joy as gathering children on a split rail fence to teach them and to learn from them.

Illustrator Cydney Bittner

Cydney Bittner received a B.A. in Studio Art and Illustration & Animation from Marymount Manhattan College. In addition to her illustration work, she has worked as an art instructor in her hometown of Bucks County, Pennsylvania. In her experience teaching, she has seen firsthand the importance of imagination; she strives to create art that nurtures that critical part of the human psyche. Cydney's other books include "Libby the Ladybug Learns Helpfulness" by Carly Furino, "George the Alligator" by Margaret Sansom and "The 7 Days" by Deborah Burns.

Printed in the USA
CPSIA information can be obtained
at www.ICGtesting.com
CBHW060548180824
13256CB00061B/609